Helen Orme taught for many years before giving up teaching to write full-time. At the last count she had written over 70 books.

She writes both fiction and non-fiction, but at present is concentrating on fiction for older readers.

Helen also runs writing workshops for children and courses for teachers in both primary and secondary schools.

How many have you read?

Stalker	978 184167 595 4
Taken for a Ride	978 184167 596 1
Odd One Out	978 184167 597 8
Lost!	978 184167 598 5
Trouble with Teachers	978 184167 599 2
Boys!	978 184167 600 5
Brother Bother	978 184167 684 5
Horsing Around	978 184167 685 2
New Man	978 184167 686 9
Who's Who?	978 184167 687 6
Wet!	978 184167 688 3
Moving	978 184167 689 0

Two years on:

Don't Do It!	978 184167 744 6
Sleepover	978 184167 741 5
She's My Friend Now	978 184167 740 8
Secrets	978 184167 743 9
Party Time	978 184167 819 1
Leave Her Alone	978 184167 742 2

Party Time

Party Time

by Helen Orme
Illustrated by Chris Askham

Published by Ransom Publishing Ltd.
Radley House, 8 St. Cross Road, Winchester, Hampshire
SO23 9HX, UK
www.ransom.co.uk

ISBN 978 184167 819 1

First published in 2011

A CIP catalogue record of this book is available from the British Library.

Meet the Sisters ...

Siti and her friends are really close. So close she calls them her Sisters. They've been mates for ever, and most of the time they are closer than her real family.

Siti is the leader – the one who always knows what to do – but Kelly, Lu, Donna and Rachel have their own lives to lead as well.

Still, there's no one you can talk to, no one you can rely on, like your best mates. Right?

Do you want to come?

Rachel was cross. Wil was going to loads of parties.

'I wish I could do something exciting,' she said.

'There's the school Christmas disco this week isn't there?' asked her mum.

'Yeah, but it's pretty boring.'

'Tell you what,' said Wil. 'I've got an invite to Jen's party. She said to take some friends. You can come with us if you want.'

'Mum,' begged Rachel. 'Can I go?'

'Well, I'm not sure,' said her mum. 'You won't know anybody there and they'll all be much older than you.'

'She'll know some of them,' said Wil. 'Wayne's coming, so are Jamie and Susie.'

Rachel looked at her mum.

'See – they'll look after me, if that's what you're worried about.'

Mum laughed. She knew that now Rachel knew Wayne was going, it would make her even more keen to go.

'All right,' she said. 'As long as Wil looks after you.'

Rachel couldn't wait to get to school the next day to tell the Sisters about it.

The Sisters were Rachel's best friends. They had known each other for years and were just as close as real sisters; maybe closer.

Donna was cross. 'How come you get to go?' she asked. 'Marie and Briony are going but they didn't ask me.'

Marie and Briony were her real older sisters.

That made Rachel cross. She really fancied Wayne and she knew he was going out with Marie. She got snappy with Donna.

'Maybe my brother thinks I'm adult enough to handle it.'

She stuck her tongue out at Donna. That made Siti laugh.

'Come on, you two,' she said. 'Neither of you stand a chance with Wayne, you should know that by now.'

'Yeah, I know,' said Donna. 'But it's not fair. It's not so much that I still fancy Wayne but I'm cross that Marie didn't ask me.'

'Oh well, maybe we can do something else instead,' said Kelly. 'We could go bowling with Gary, Simon and Billy.'

Lu pulled a face at Kelly. 'Maybe,' she said. 'Maybe not.'

2

Not much fun

Rachel spent a long time getting ready for the party. She'd managed to get some money from her mum for a new dress. She put her make-up on carefully.

She looked at least 18, she thought. She was really looking forward to it. Maybe she could make Wayne look at her like a real woman, not just his friend's kid sister.

The party was at Jen's house. Mum had dropped them both off.

‘Do you want me to pick you up?’ she asked.

‘No, someone will give us a lift home,’ said Wil.

‘Just be careful then,’ said mum. ‘And look after Rachel.’

‘Yeah, no probs,’ said Wil. ‘See you later.’

It started to go wrong as soon as they got inside.

Jen looked Rachel up and down.

'Who's this?' she demanded.

'My kid sister. Rachel, meet Jen.'

Jen waved at a corner of the room.

'Booze is over there, food's in the kitchen.' She grabbed Wil by the arm and pulled him away.

'She fancies him,' thought Rachel. 'I don't like her much.'

She looked round the room. There was Wayne. She started to move over towards him but he hadn't seen her. Wayne had his arm round Marie and, as she watched, they started snogging. She couldn't go over now.

Who else was there that she could talk to? Everyone else was in little groups. She couldn't just go and push in. She was beginning to wish she hadn't come.

She looked for Wil. At least she could go and talk to him. But she couldn't see him anywhere.

The music was very loud; she was beginning to get a headache. She wandered out to the kitchen. She might as well get something to eat at least.

3

Things get better

There were a couple of guys in the kitchen when she went in. They looked her up and down.

'Hi, I'm Tom,' he grinned at her. 'And this is Jimmy.'

Rachel recognised Jimmy. He was one of Wil's friends.

Rachel smiled back at him. Maybe it wasn't so bad here after all.

'Grab something to eat,' said Tom, 'and come and get a drink. What do you want?'

Rachel thought fast. She didn't drink much.

'What have they got?' she asked.

'Everything,' he said. 'Come on I'll get you something good.'

He put his arm round her and took her back into the other room.

'How come I haven't seen you around before?'

He picked up a bottle and started pouring.

'Not too much.' Rachel took the glass.

'I came with Wil.' She didn't want to explain that she was Wil's sister. She wanted Tom to think she was his girlfriend or something.

'Well he's not around so that's cool,' he said. 'I've got time to get to know you really well.'

It would have been great – if it hadn't been for the booze. As soon as Rachel's glass was empty, Tom filled it again.

Rachel began to feel very hot.

'I need to go outside for a bit,' she said.

She turned towards the front door. Tom moved to follow her but somehow someone else got in the way. The someone was Wil. He didn't look happy.

'Where do you think you're going?'

He glared at Tom. 'You leave my sister alone.'

Tom shrugged, 'She didn't say she was your sister. Anyway she can make up her own mind what to do.'

He put his arm round Rachel, 'Come on babe, he can go and ...'

Wil pulled Tom's arm away. 'I said leave her alone. She's only 15.'

Rachel sank down to the floor. 'I'm going to throw up,' she gasped.

4

Things get worse

Wil bent over. ‘Come on, get up,’ he said. ‘It’s time to go home.’

Jen came over.

‘Do something about her. She can’t be sick in here.’

Wil picked her up and dragged her towards the door. Jen opened it.

When the cold air hit Rachel, that was it.

She bent over a rose bush, groaning.

'I feel awful. I can't go home on the bus.'

'You don't need to, Jimmy's going to take us. He's just passed his test so he said he'd give a few of us a lift back. He's got his dad's car.'

Wil called across the room.

'Jim, when will you be ready to go?'

Jimmy came over. He looked at Rachel, who was sitting on the doorstep.

'Sorry mate. I can't have her in the car. If she's sick my old man will kill me.'

Wil swore. 'I'll have to get a cab then.'

'A cab driver won't take you either,' said Jen. 'They won't take people as drunk as she is.'

'There's only one thing left,' said Wil, pulling a face. 'It will have to be Mum.'

He looked down at Rachel. 'You know what Mum'll say about this, don't you?'

Rachel groaned. 'It wasn't my fault. It was Tom. He kept giving me drinks.'

Wil looked round the room. He'd let Tom know just what he thought about guys who messed with his sister.

But Tom had already gone. He'd left with Jimmy and a couple of girls. They'd taken a couple of bottles with them. Maybe they could carry on with the party somewhere else.

Wil rang their mum. She was not pleased.

Rachel looked awful and she felt awful. She knew Wil wasn't going to forgive her in a hurry!

5

Not so bad after all

The drive home was just as awful as Rachel had thought. First Mum had a go at her, then she had a go at Wil. So then Wil got stroppy with Mum.

'It wasn't my fault. How was I to know she'd keep drinking like that?'

'But I only had a couple,' mumbled Rachel. She wished they'd shut up. She didn't feel quite so sick, but her head hurt and she wanted to go to sleep.

She didn't remember much more. Mum put her to bed as soon as they got home.

Sunday was pretty bad too. More nagging from both Mum and Wil. And she was grounded until Christmas. She called Siti and told her she couldn't see the Sisters.

'I'll tell you all about it tomorrow in school,' she promised. In a way she was quite glad not to go out – she still didn't feel too good.

By Monday she was feeling better, even if Mum was still going on. She was even looking forward to telling the others about it all.

But when she walked into the form room she could see they were all talking about something else.

She walked over to them.

'Have you heard?' asked Donna.

'Heard what?'

'After the party. Jimmy smashed up his dad's car.'

Rachel went white. She and Wil might have been in the car with Jimmy.

'Are they all right?'

'Yeah, sort of,' said Donna. 'They were lucky. The car's a write-off but they all got out.'

'Jimmy hadn't been drinking,' said Kelly, 'but the police found booze in the car so he's being charged with dangerous driving.'

'Marie said they were all fooling around when they left,' put in Donna. 'They had this guy Tom with them. She said he's a real idiot. He always drinks too much.'

'Drinking too much isn't a good idea,' said Rachel slowly, thinking about what her mum had said.

'But maybe this time it wasn't so bad after all.'